For

From

Date

ISBN 0-8249-5489-0

First published in this format in 2004 by Ideals Children's Books
An imprint of Ideals Publications
A division of Guideposts
535 Metroplex Drive, Suite 250
Nashville, Tennessee 37211
www.idealsbooks.com

Previously published by Lang Books, Delafield, Wisconsin

Library of Congress CIP data on file

Printed and bound in Italy

3 5 7 9 10 8 6 4 2

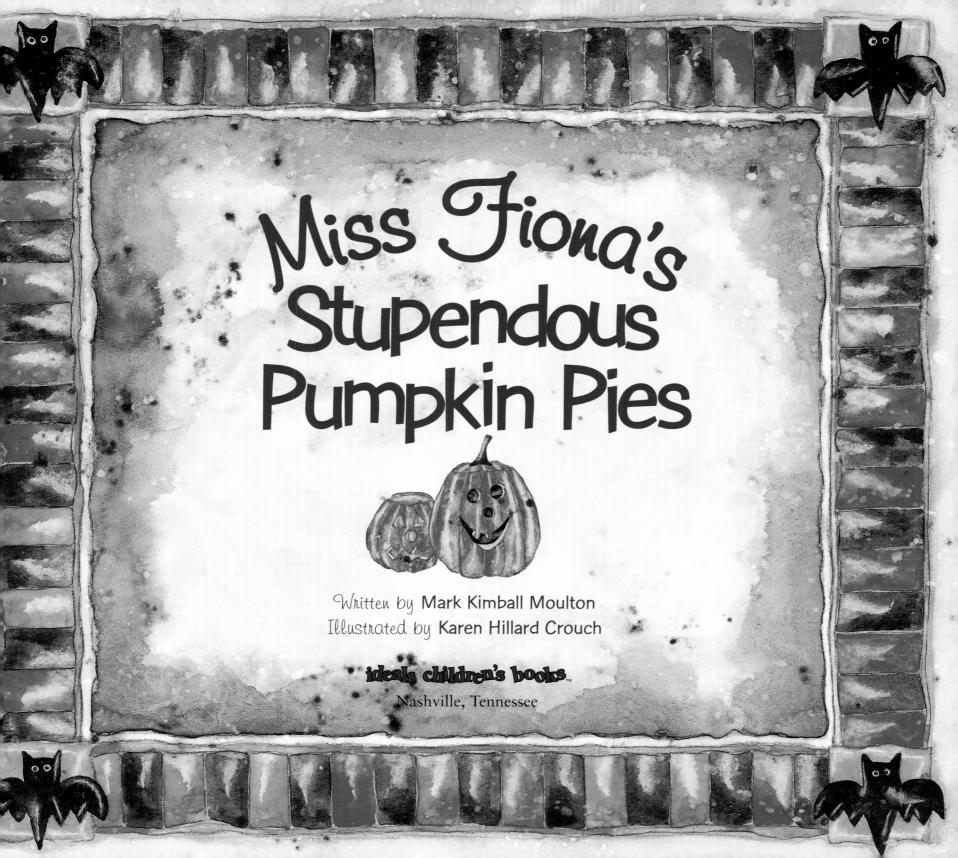

Miss Fiona's Stupendous Pumpkin Pies

Written by **Mark Kimball Moulton**
Illustrated by **Karen Hillard Crouch**

ideals children's books™

Nashville, Tennessee

Down past the spooky graveyard
and across the stubbled fields,
there lies a big, old haunted house
where all the paint has peeled.

The shutters on the windows
hang crooked, if at all.
The roof is in such bad repair
it looks like it might fall.

There's a stone wall in the side yard
and a crooked picket fence.
An old barn sits behind the house
that isn't worth two cents!

In the garden there's a scarecrow
with his stuffing falling out.
And everywhere you look, you see
stray cats lying about.

This house appears deserted,
but it is still occupied
(although some believe its
occupants can disappear and fly)!

The old woman, Miss Fiona,
lives here with all her cats.
A horse and cow live in the barn,
along with several bats.

Now legend says Fiona
is four hundred years and three,
though she never looked
much older than
   two hundred years to me!

She walks a bit stooped over
and wears a long, black dress.
And underneath
her pointed hat,
her hair's a stringy mess!

One eye is larger
than the other,
there's a big wart
on her nose,
        and on her feet
            are bright red shoes
                with doodads
                    on the toes!

Some folks think she's kooky,
dressed like a witch on Halloween,
but that just proves appearances
aren't always what they seem.

For she keeps a tidy garden
with a good-sized pumpkin patch,
and every Halloween she serves
fresh pumpkin pie from scratch.

Sometime in late October
Miss Fiona starts her yield
and brings in all her pumpkins
from her big ol' pumpkin field.

Pumpkins line her windowsills
and pumpkins line her floor—
she has so many pumpkins, some
come rolling out the door!

She keeps pumpkins in her attic
and some in her woodshed.
There are even some who'll tell you
she keeps pumpkins in her bed!

Then, on the day of Halloween,
and not one day before,
Fiona gathers all her pumpkins
and begins her yearly chore.

She hangs a cauldron on the fire
to bubble and to boil.
She chops and peels
and rolls and stirs
in a frenzied baking toil.

Now and then she'll cackle
as she checks her recipe;
then she'll peek
over her shoulder
to make sure no one sees.

For her ingredients
are secret,
but as she sets
each pie to cool,
the spicy scent that fills the air
makes everybody drool!

No matter how you beg and plead, Fiona holds her ground.
Not one piece of pie is served till midnight rolls around!

As angels, spooks, and goblins
start to gather in the street,
the night is filled with laughter
and the cries of "Trick or treat!"

Black cats and ballerinas
run to each house and in-between,
wishing every witch and ghost
a "Happy Halloween!"

But the last house that we visit,
as the midnight hour draws nigh,
is down past the spooky graveyard
for a slice of pumpkin pie!

Boys and girls for miles around
come knocking at her door,
dressed in such frightful costumes
as vampires or dinosaurs.

Miss Fiona shrieks and giggles
as she welcomes each new guest,
then sends them to the backyard
to wait with all the rest.

As the witching hour creeps closer,
Fiona steps out on her porch,
with a crow upon her shoulder,
in her hand, a burning torch.

She surveys all of her visitors,
and we wave and smile to greet her.
Then she slowly lets her spooky gaze
fall on one special trick-or-treater.

She points and crooks her finger
and wiggles her eyebrows,
then cackles:

"Come, my dearie, I need
help inside my house."

This year it's a pink rabbit
that is Miss Fiona's choice—
we all look at her with envy,
all the little girls and boys.

For it's quite the supreme honor
to help Fiona serve her pies—
a most distinguished, rare
accomplishment, to be so recognized!

The seconds tick by slowly. . . .
The anticipation grows. . . .
The moon peeks out behind the clouds.
The wind begins to blow.

Then, far off in the distance,
the church bells begin to peal,
and from inside her kitchen,
we hear Miss Fiona squeal.

With that, Fiona's helper
throws the front door open wide
and beckons every girl and boy
to come and step inside.

The house is warm and cozy,
with carved pumpkins everywhere
(though you do have to be careful
not to get cobwebs in your hair)!

Owls hoot in the pantry.
Cats lie at Fiona's feet.
From upstairs we hear wails and moans
that make Halloween complete!

The pies are most delicious,
and she also serves warm cider.
Then she passes out souvenir rings
in the shape of creepy spiders!

And after every one of us has had cider
and been fed, she tells us spooky stories
that make our eyes pop from our heads!

And as we leave, she sends us home
with an extra slice of pie
for Mom and Dad and Grandma, who wait up till we arrive.

Most folks are very curious about Fiona and her ways,
but mostly it's her pumpkin pies we talk about for days!

I must admit, Fiona's kooky, with her warts and pale green skin;
but who cares how kooky someone looks
when there's goodness deep within!

Still, I scratch my head and wonder
when folks ask the secret to her pie—
'cause she'll wink and snort and cackle
to everyone's surprise:

"Just take one big, plump,
ripe pumpkin;
add a lizard and a toad.
Stir in
a few
good
bat
wings…

"and serve it a' la mode!"

The End